Usborne

ZOO

Sticker & Colouring Book

Illustrated by Cecilia Johansson
and Candice Whatmore

Designed by Claire Ever,
Francesca Allen and Matt Durber

Words by Sam Taplin and
Jessica Greenwell

You'll find all the stickers
in the middle of the book.

Lions and tigers

These people have come to see the big cats.
Add some lions and tigers to the picture.

TIGERS

African animals

Giraffes, hippos and rhinos live in this part of the zoo. Stick lots of them on.

Playful elephants

Elephants love playing in the water. Stick a baby elephant and some big elephants around the waterfall.

Penguins and seals

It's feeding time. Add some hungry
penguins and seals to the picture.

SEALS

Snakes and lizards

Lots of snakes and lizards live here.
Put each one in the right place.

Coral snake

Thorny devil

Boa

Iguana

Frilled lizard

Chameleon

Gecko

9

Rainforest birds

Beautiful birds from rainforests flap through these trees. Fill the birdhouse with them.

In the aquarium

All kinds of different fish swim around in the aquarium.
Find a shark and lots of tropical fish to put in the water.

Chimpanzees

Chimpanzees are very good at climbing.
Add some chimps swinging through the trees.

Children's zoo

Children come here to meet the farm animals.
Add a pony, a cow and some baby animals.

16

Lions and tigers (pages 2 and 3)

Tigers
and cubs

Lions and
cubs

African animals (pages 4 and 5)

Hippos

Zebras

Gazelles

Giraffes

Ostriches

Rhinos

Playful elephants (pages 6 and 7)

Indian elephants

Penguins and seals (page 8)

Penguins

Seals

Snakes and lizards (page 9)

Boa

Thorny devil

Iguana

Gecko

Coral
snake

Chameleon

Frilled lizard

Rainforest birds (pages 10 and 11)

Toucans

Different kinds
of parrots

Hummingbirds

In the aquarium (pages 12 and 13)

Sea turtle

Rays

Sea horses

Tropical fish

Reef shark

Chimpanzees (pages 14 and 15)

Children's zoo (page 16)

Lambs

Cow

Goose and goslings

Rabbits

Duck and ducklings

Goat and kid

Hen and chicks

Eggs

Miniature pony

Children with feed

Girl with feed

Use these stickers on pages 18-31, if you like.

Use these stickers on page 32.

Colouring

In this part of the book,
there are lots of pictures to colour.
There are also some stickers to add
to the pages. You'll find them in
the middle of the book.

Lions and monkeys

Colour this lion family relaxing in the sun and the monkeys swinging in the tree.

Giraffes and elephants

Colour the hungry giraffes and the playful
elephants splashing in the water.

Penguins and dolphins

Colour the dolphins, and the penguins waiting for treats.

Camels and hippos

Colour two kinds of camels, and some hippos too.

Sea creatures

The aquarium is full of amazing sea creatures.
Use lots of colours to bring them to life.

The reptile house

What colours could slithering snakes,
lazy lizards and grumpy frogs be?

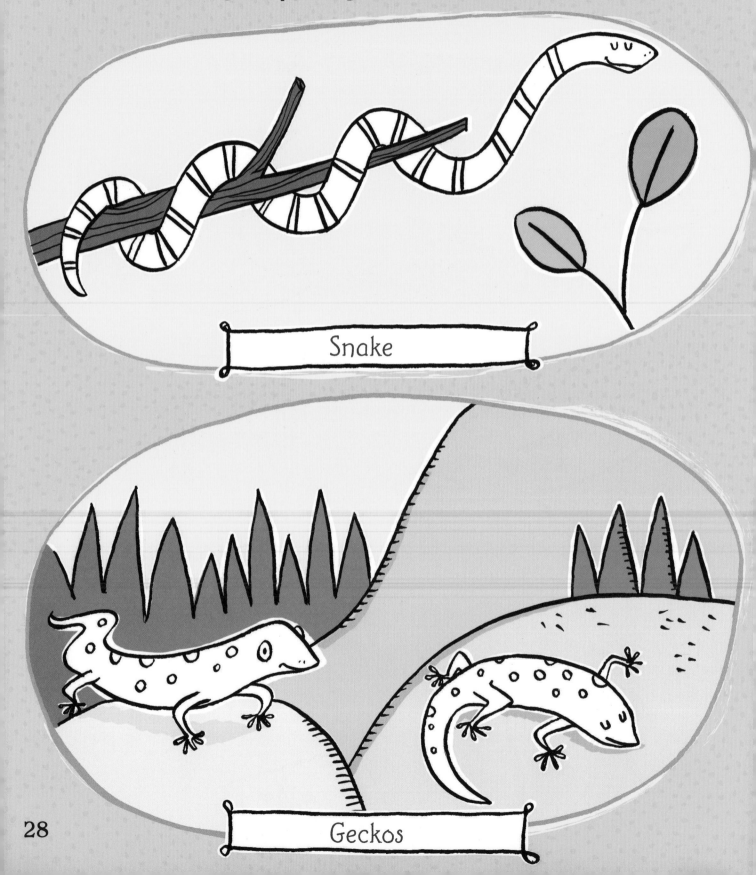

Snake

Geckos

Tree frogs

Chameleon

The birdhouse

Colourful birds flap, paddle and perch in the birdhouse. Colour all of them.

Find the stickers to match these pictures.

Dolphin

Flamingo

Camel

Elephant

Monkey

Snake

Tree frog

Hippo

Lion

Turtle

Penguin

Parrot

Giraffe

Shark